For my sistras, Blue and Fee,

two of my dearest friends – E.A.

For Nathan and Charlotte x – M.B.

First American Edition 2022
Kane Miller, A Division of EDC Publishing

Text copyright © Emma Adams, 2021
Illustrations copyright © Mike Byrne, 2021
The moral rights of Emma Adams and Mike Byrne have been asserted.
First published in 2021 by Scholastic Children's Books, a division of Scholastic Ltd
Euston House, 24 Eversholt Street, London NW1 1DB

Library of Congress Control Number: 2021937040

Printed and bound in China
1 2 3 4 5 6 7 8 9 10

ISBN: 978-1-68464-375-2

FSC
www.fsc.org
MIX
Paper from
responsible sources
FSC® C008047

EMMA ADAMS   MIKE BYRNE

UNICORNS DON'T LOVE RAINBOWS

Kane Miller
A DIVISION OF EDC PUBLISHING

So many unicorns love to be **happy**,
they spend their days **smiling**
– well, I think that's **sappy**.

Yes, I **am** a unicorn, but
(as you'll see)
there really is something
quite **different**
about me.

Because . . .

I do not like smiling,

I do not like cake,

I do not like ice cream
(makes my
tummy ache).

I **stomp** over rainbows

and will **not** say
"WHOOP!"

(and **don't** talk to me
about unicorn poop).

My unicorn friends love to **gallop** through flowers,

then lie making daisy chains
(literally, for hours).

They brew petal perfume,
"DELIGHTFUL!"
they cry

(when I have a sniff, something gets in my eye).

They all **love** bright colors – **especially** pink,
but this in particular makes my heart sink.

For, I have a style that most unicorns lack,
and that is because my favorite color is ...

. . . black!

I love black on everything and everywhere,
my clothes and my bedroom – it's all black in there!

If I'm wearing black, then I **never** feel gray,
but when my friends see me ... they all run away.

Because . . .

My friends **love** rainbows –
they **love** every color

(but they **don't** love black
because it makes them feel duller).

They paint rainbow paintings and say it's the norm,
but when I paint mine...

"What IS it?"

"...It's a storm."

Also...

They **love** the sun, but I love when it's pouring –
thunder and lightning? That never gets boring!

They glitter and sparkle,
from heads to their toes,

they go to bed early
– well, that's just **not** right!

And when it gets dark,
when the day turns to night,

They **love** karaoke

and I love that too,

but the songs that I like
aren't the ones that they do.

but glitter's **SO** itchy
– as everyone knows.

Suddenly, I realize with a **puff**,
we think differently about all sorts of stuff.

Should I only have friends who think like I do?

Who only like black
(and who hate rainbow poo)?

No!

I can be **me**, and **you** can be **you** –

and we can help others to feel that way too.

For, here is the most helpful thing you will find,

the best thing in life is to **always** be kind.

So if you want a friend, you won't have to go far,
and people will **love you** the way that you are.

Remember: your friends can be quite unlike you,
so we **can** be different ...
and similar too!